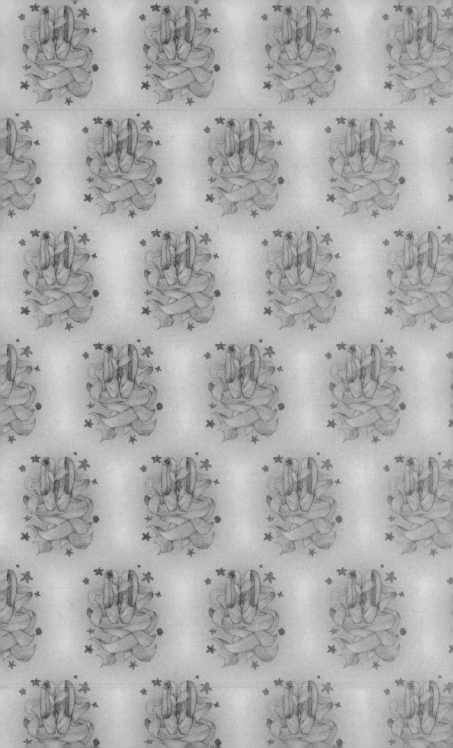

This book belongs to

_____

Sugarplum
Mines

The
Lake

Zuckerbrote
Peak

Drosselmeyer Pl

The Western Frostings

Donkey's Causeway

The
Rocks

Dross

The

Rocky
Falls

King
Caspar's
Mines

Rushing River

Leopard's
Paradise

The City   The

Forest

The Eastern Frosting

...meyer Plains

Valley

R. Verbena

Toffee-Apple
Orchards

FALKNER 2003

*Look out for all the Kingdom
of the Frosty Mountains books!*

KINGDOM OF THE FROSTY MOUNTAINS

Ursula of the Boughs

Emerald Everhart

Illustrated by
Patricia Ann Lewis-MacDougall

EGMONT

EGMONT

We bring stories to life

Ursula of the Boughs first published in 2008
by Egmont UK Limited
239 Kensington High Street
London W8 6SA

Text copyright © 2008 Angela Woolfe
Illustrations copyright © 2008 Patricia Ann Lewis-MacDougall

The moral rights of the author and illustrator have been asserted

ISBN 978 1 4052 3330 9

1 3 5 7 9 10 8 6 4 2

A CIP catalogue record for this title is available from the British Library

Printed and bound in Italy by L.E.G.O. S.P.A

Contents

Prologue

When I was a young Ballerina, an admirer gave me a gift.

It was only a frosted-glass perfume bottle, filled with a sweet scent of lemon and orange. But my admirer told me that

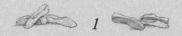

the bottle was the most precious thing he could give, because there was a magical Kingdom inside.

I didn't believe him at first.

But that night, I had a very special dream. I dreamed of a magical Kingdom, the most beautiful land I'd ever seen, filled with delightful people and their very special animals. And the next time I danced, I thought of the Kingdom, and suddenly I danced as I had never danced before. Every night that I wore the perfume, I danced

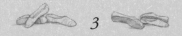

better than ever, until I was the most famous Ballerina in the world.

But one day, the old frosted-glass bottle was accidentally thrown away.

And from that day onwards, I never danced so beautifully again.

I searched for the bottle high and low, but I never found it. I have since had many years to write down what I learned about the Kingdom inside . . .

Inside the bottle, behind snow-capped Frosty Mountains, the Kingdom is divided

into five parts. There are frozen Lakes in the north, warmer meadows in the southern Valley, stark grey Rocks in the west, and to the east, a deep, dark Forest.

And the City. How could I forget the City? Silverberg, the capital, rising from the

Drosselmeyer Plains like a beautiful new jewel on an old ring.

From a distance, the houses seem to be piled on top of each other. Their brightly painted wooden roofs look as if they hold up the floors of the dwellings above as they wind around and around ever-more-narrow streets. And at the very top of the teetering pile is the biggest building of all: the Royal Palace. It is made from snow-white marble taken from the Frosty Mountains themselves, which glows in the *early morning sun and sparkles in the cold night.*

The Royal Palace is the home of the King and Queen. But it is here too, within

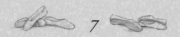

the marble walls of the Palace, that you can find the Kingdom's famous Royal Ballet School. This is where the most talented young Ballerinas in the land become proper Ballerinas-in-Training, and really learn to dance. They travel from far and wide. Pale blonde Lake girls journey from the north, dark-haired Valley Dwellers come from the south. Grey-eyed Ballerinas travel from the western Rocks, and green-eyed Forest girls make their way from the east. The City girls have no need to come quite so far.

Of course, they all bring their pets. Each Kingdom Dweller has their own animal companion. And these animals can talk — talk just like you and me. Lake Dwellers keep Arctic foxes or snow leopards, while Valley Dwellers keep small tigers, monkeys or exotic birds. Strong, sturdy Rock Dwellers enjoy the company of sheep, goats and donkeys, while Forest Dwellers keep black bears and leopards. Every City Dweller keeps an eagle.

Out there, somewhere, is my old

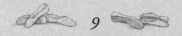

frosted-glass perfume bottle.

Out there, somewhere, are the Ballerinas-in-Training who inspired me – Jessica Juniper, Crystal Coldwater, Laura-Bella Bergamotta, Valentina de la Frou and Ursula of the Boughs.

And they will wait for you, until the day that you find them.

Emerald Everhart

CHAPTER ONE
The Story of the Missing Princess

It was the summer term at the Royal Ballet School, and close to the end of the school year. The days were longer and the nights were lighter. The sun shone so brightly that even the hardest frost on the city's roofs began to soften and almost melt.

In the Beginners' dormitory one night, the girls' pink-and-gold quilts were too warm to sleep under, so Jessica Juniper and her friends crept out of their beds after lights-out, and went to sit beside the open window. They told stories until they were shivering in their pyjamas, and longing to crawl under their quilts again. At first they took it in turns to tell stories about their homes.

Jessica spun a wonderful fairy tale about a magical Rock Dweller. Crys told a scary story about a ghost at the Lake. Laura-Bella made them all laugh with a silly story about her home in the Valley. Valentina talked mostly about the wonderful shops near her house in the smartest part of the City. And Ursula . . .

Well, Ursula did not want to tell a story at all.

'Come on, Ursula! There are some

amazing fairy tales from the Forest,'
said Jessica, trying to encourage her
quiet friend.

'I'd really rather not,' Ursula begged,
hiding behind her long dark fringe, and

looking even more nervous than usual. 'I much prefer to listen.'

'Let Ursula do what she wants!' said Sinbad, Jessica's donkey, who had seen an opportunity. 'If she'd rather listen, well, she can listen to me! I've got a *brilliant* story.'

Everyone sighed, apart from Olympia, Valentina's eagle, who loved Sinbad's long, exciting stories.

'Settle down, everyone,' commanded Sinbad, 'and listen to the story of The

Missing Princess.'

'But Sinbad, *everybody* at school knows that story,' said Jessica.

'*I* don't,' said Crys, who never kept up to date with the Palace gossip.

'The story goes that King Caspar and Queen Mab's only daughter, Princess Coppelia, ran away with a musician ten years ago and never returned,' Jessica explained. 'The King and Queen never spoke of her again. It's more of a rumour than a story.'

'Not the way *I* was going to tell it.' Sinbad's ears drooped. 'I was going to put in goblins, and pirate ships, and everything.'

'Well, I'm bored with fairy stories, goblins and pirate ships and all,' said Valentina, tossing her long, strawberry blonde hair. 'Can't we talk about the end-of-year concert? That's *much* more exciting.'

'It's true,' said Laura-Bella, who was curled up beside her small tiger,

Mr Melchior, for warmth. As a Valley Dweller, she would rather have been in her cosy bed by now. 'It's the first time our families will all come to the school, and see us dance here. I can't wait to show my mum and dad around the whole school –'

She stopped talking at a sudden strange noise from Ursula.

The quiet Forest Dweller had started crying.

'Ursula, what's wrong?' They all

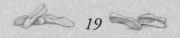

crowded around, but Ursula only hid behind her hair, unable to speak.

'We had a letter from Ursula's dad today,' said Dorothea, Ursula's pet bear, in her soft voice. 'He has far too many orders for violins, and he's so busy that he can't come to the end-of-year concert.'

Everyone fell silent. They all knew how much Ursula loved her father, one of the finest musical-instrument makers in the Kingdom. Her mother had died when Ursula was just a little baby, so her dad was all she had. And now he was not even going to be able to come and watch her dance in the concert!

'Don't worry, Ursula,' said Jessica, trying to comfort her friend. 'You can help show *my* family around the school . . .'

'It won't be the same,' wept Ursula. 'I just wanted my dad to come and see me dance in the concert, that's all.'

Later that night, after Ursula had

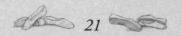

finally gone to sleep, clutching
Dorothea, her friends gathered around
Jessica's bed to talk.

'How *dare* Ursula's dad be so
thoughtless!' said Laura-Bella.

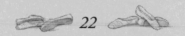

'He can't help it if he has to work very hard,' said Crys, repeating the wise words her pet white fox, Pollux, had just whispered in her ear. 'I'm sure he'd love to be here.'

But Laura-Bella was having none of it. 'I've a good mind to tell him just what I think of him and his violin orders!'

'That's it!' said Jessica. 'We can write her dad a letter.'

'Brilliant!' Sinbad waggled his ears so wildly that his hat fell off. 'Oooh, we'll write the rudest, stinkiest letter he's ever seen.'

'No,' said Jessica firmly. 'We'll write a nice, polite letter, but we'll tell him that everybody else will have their families here and that poor Ursula would like that, too.'

They found a pencil and a notebook, and sat up late into the night writing the letter.

It went off in the post-carriage first thing the next morning.

CHAPTER TWO
News for Ursula

Two weeks passed, and still there was no reply from Ursula's father.

It was hard for Ursula to enjoy the rehearsals for the end-of-year concert. She could hardly bring herself to feel happy even when she was given the lead part of the Ugly Duckling in one of the Beginners' dances. The others did their best to keep her cheerful, and kept quiet about their own parents' visits to Silverberg. But as the last week of term came along, they knew they would not be able to hide their families' plans any more.

'Ursula, why don't you come with me and Sinbad to meet my mum and dad and brothers and sisters at the West

Gate?' suggested Jessica over breakfast on the day of the concert. 'They've heard so much about you from my letters, it's like you're a member of the family already!'

'Thanks, Jess,' said Ursula quietly. 'But I think I'll just stay here and practise my solo.'

'Post is here, girls!' came Mistress Hawthorne's booming voice, as she passed up and down the tables handing out letters. 'Here's one for you, Ursula!'

Ursula's hands were trembling as she

read the envelope. 'It's my dad's handwriting . . .'

'Open it up!' said Dorothea the bear.

Everyone at the table crossed their fingers very tightly, hoping as hard as they could that it would be good news.

'He says he can come after all!' Ursula dropped the letter into Sinbad's Raspberry Flancakes, but he was so pleased that he hardly minded. 'He can't be away from his workshop for very long, but he'll be here just before the concert

starts, he promises.' Her green eyes sparkled. 'And he says I should say hello to my friends, and invite you all to come and stay in the Forest for a week in the summer holidays.'

Jessica and the others were relieved that Ursula had not noticed their meddling, and that her father had not minded it.

'This is going to be the best day ever,' declared Ursula, giving Dorothea a kiss on the nose. 'I can't wait for the concert now!'

It was a busy, exciting day for everyone, as their families arrived in Silverberg and were shown around the Palace. For some, like Crys's mother, who had been a very famous Ballerina in her young days, and Valentina, whose father worked as a courtier for the King, it was nothing new. But for Jessica and Laura-Bella's families the tour around the huge, golden Palace was thrilling. Added to this was the special tea laid on by the headmistress of the school, Mistress Odette. Every kind of sandwich and cake that could be imagined was laid out on long, pink-linen-covered tables in the Great Hall.

Jessica's seven brothers and sisters and
their pet sheep and goats ate far too
many cakes, encouraged by Sinbad, and

had to be taken away to lie down before
the concert began. But even the nasty
smirks of Rubellina Goodfellow and her

father the Chancellor could not ruin the girls' day. Before they even knew it, Mistress Camomile was telling them to go and put their costumes on for the concert.

'My father still isn't here,' fretted Ursula. 'If he doesn't arrive soon, he won't get a seat.'

'I know – let's tell someone to keep a really good seat for him.' Jessica could see Master Silas, the History of Ballet teacher, walking towards the Theatre. 'Master Silas, can we ask you to keep a spare seat for Ursula's dad?'

'Of course,' said Master Silas, with a smile. 'I'll hold a seat right next to mine. Now, what does your father look like, Ursula, so I'll know when I see him?'

Ursula was terribly shy in the presence of her teachers, and mumbled down at her shoes, 'He'll be wearing a green cloak.'

'There are a lot of Forest Dwellers

in green cloaks here today!' said Master Silas.

Ursula blushed. 'Yes, of course . . . well, the best way to recognise him is that although he's a Forest Dweller, he doesn't have green eyes like all the rest of us. As a matter of fact, his eyes are blue.'

Master Silas stared at her. 'What did you say?'

'He's a blue-eyed Forest Dweller,' said Jessica, helping Ursula out. 'Thank you very much, Master Silas – now, we really have to go and get dressed.'

Master Silas stared after them as they hurried away. He had turned very pale, and his hands were shaking.

'The blue-eyed Forest Dweller is coming back,' he murmured. 'After all this time . . .'

CHAPTER THREE
The Blue-Eyed Forest Dweller

The concert was a huge success. No one was clapped and cheered more noisily than the Beginners, who performed three separate dances. The last of these was the *Ugly Duckling* ballet, with Ursula in the lead role. As she peeked out from the wings before coming onstage, she could just see her father in the second row of the audience.

'He made it!' she whispered to her friends, who gave her huge grins. She did not think she had ever felt so happy.

The second party of the day was after the show, in the Winter Garden. By the time Ursula and her friends had changed out of their beautiful costumes and scrubbed off their stage make-up, the

party was already in full swing. Across the Garden, Ursula could see her father, talking very seriously with Master Silas.

'Probably saying what a terrible pupil you are,' Laura-Bella teased.

As she went closer, Ursula began to worry that Laura-Bella's joke might be true. Her father's thin face was creased with a frown, and Master Silas looked more serious than ever. Their heads were very close together, and they were speaking in low voices.

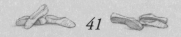

'What's going on?' Dorothea whispered in Ursula's ear. 'Do you think we're in trouble?'

'I don't know,' Ursula said, 'but it's strange. The way they're talking, it looks almost as if they *know* each other.'

Suddenly, there came a loud fanfare. The Seventeen Royal Flugelhorn players marched through the huge golden doors, their famous Musical Eagles on their shoulders. The sweet voices of the Musical Eagles were singing the national anthem, which meant only one thing. The King and Queen were making a surprise visit to the party.

Chancellor Godwin Goodfellow led the Royal Procession, gazing about the Winter Garden with his sharp black eyes. Next came Queen Mab, who wore so many necklaces and earrings that it seemed a wonder she could hold her head upright. She gave a little wave here and there before snapping at the King to catch up. King Caspar wandered in at the back, almost as though he had lost his way out in the corridor. His Frosting-Stone crown was rather wonky, and his glorious red robes a little too tight. He beamed around at the crowds, delighted to walk amongst his subjects.

'Hello, there . . . er . . . Loyal Subject. Nice to see you . . . er . . . Loyal Subject. Good evening . . . er . . . I'm sorry,' he apologised to one member of the crowd, 'I don't know your name.' He wandered on. 'Welcome, welcome . . .

er . . . Loyal Subject . . .'

Suddenly, there was a terrible shriek from the Queen, and the whole Garden fell silent.

'What is *that man* doing here?'

Her shaking finger was pointing towards Ursula's father.

King Caspar's beam vanished. 'Good heavens,' he croaked. 'It's the Blue-Eyed Forest Dweller.'

Chancellor Goodfellow's eyes gleamed brighter than ever. 'Guards! Arrest that man!' he snapped.

Four of the Chancellor's guards ran forward and seized Ursula's father.

'No!' Ursula tried to stop them, but

it was too late.

'Ursula,' her father called, seeing her for the first time. 'It's all right –'

'It most certainly is *not* all right!' screamed the Queen. 'How dare you come back here, Forest Dweller! How dare you come back, when the last time you stole Princess Coppelia away from us!'

Everybody in the Garden let out a gasp.

'I did not steal your daughter,' said

Ursula's father in a low, calm voice. He looked towards the King. 'Coppelia and I loved each other. When she knew I was leaving the Palace with the other musicians in my orchestra, she begged to come back to the Forest with me.' He bowed his head. 'Now she is dead, and I miss her every day of my life.'

'Take him away!' Chancellor Goodfellow shouted.

Ursula felt as though the floor had been turned into jelly beneath her feet.

'Please let him go,' she begged, pulling at the King's cloak. 'He's my father.'

King Caspar blinked at her. 'Ah. Then do you know who I am?'

'You're the King.'

'Um . . . that's right, my dear,' said the King. 'But I am something else, too. It appears that I am also . . . um . . . your grandfather.'

'Darling!' Queen Mab swept Ursula into her arms, covering her with extremely wet tears. 'A pupil at the school

all this time! What is your name?'

'I'm just Ursula,' said Ursula in a
very, very small voice indeed.

'Not any more,' muttered the Chancellor through gritted teeth. He gave the Royal Flugelhorns a signal for a fanfare. 'All hail,' he announced, 'to her Most High Majesty – the *Princess Ursula*.'

Ursula could see her friends' astonished faces across the Winter Garden. But there was no time to say anything to them, for the very next moment, the King and Queen were leading her and Dorothea away, through

the huge gold doors and into the Royal
Palace.

CHAPTER FOUR
A New Princess

That night, Ursula's four best friends and their pets huddled together by the big window in the dormitory, whispering in the darkness.

'Poor Ursula!' Jessica's teeth were

chattering in the chilly night air.

'*Poor* Ursula?' Valentina said. 'She's a princess, Jessica! What could be more exciting than that?'

'Don't be so silly, Val,' said Crys crossly. 'Her father was dragged away by the guards before her very eyes! *That* can't have been very exciting.'

'I heard some of the servants' pets gossiping in the kitchens,' Sinbad said. 'They said Ursula's dad is being held a prisoner by Chancellor Goodfellow.'

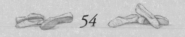

'A prisoner!' Laura-Bella was in tears. 'This is terrible.'

Even Valentina was starting to look concerned. 'But surely the King and Queen will be looking after Ursula. She's their granddaughter, after all.'

'If they harm a patch of fur on Dorothea's head . . .' began Sinbad, then burst into noisy tears himself.

'Calm down, everyone,' said Mr Melchior, Laura-Bella's tiger. He gave them all a stern look that could not quite

hide his own worries. 'Ursula and Dorothea are perfectly safe. They're probably in the most beautiful bedroom in the whole Palace, being fed Raspberry Flancakes from a golden platter.'

Sinbad stopped sobbing, and looked rather jealous.

'You're probably quite right, Mr Melchior,' said Jessica sensibly. 'We'll speak to Mistress Odette in the morning, and ask if we can go to the Palace to see Ursula . . . I mean, *Princess* Ursula.' The new name felt strange on Jessica's lips.

The next morning, the whole Banqueting Hall was buzzing with the news. Jessica and her friends gobbled their breakfasts, not meeting anyone's eye. They were just hurrying off to Mistress Odette's study when Rubellina Goodfellow blocked their way.

'Rubellina, this is no time for your nasty comments,' Jessica sighed. 'Please let us past.'

'Jessica! How could you think I was going to be nasty to you?' Rubellina's blue eyes were wide and innocent. 'I was just going to invite you all to come and sit at our table.' She pointed over to her usual table, where she always sat with her rich, spiteful City Dweller friends.

'No, thanks,' said Jessica.

But Rubellina tried to link arms. 'I thought it would be nice if we could all start being friends, now that we're moving up into Better-than-Beginners.'

'You mean you thought it would be nice if you could make friends with a princess,' said Jessica, pulling her arm away.

Rubellina lost her smile and broke into a dreadful scowl. 'Why don't you

just shut up, you scummy little Rock Dweller? Princess Ursula won't want to be friends with you lot any more. Now that she's royalty, she'll make friends with the right kind of girls, you wait and see.'

'You don't think Rubellina's right, do you?' Jessica whispered to Crys, as the four girls and their pets stood waiting for Mistress Odette outside her study. 'About Ursula not wanting to be our friend now?'

'Not in the least,' said Crys. 'Ursula will always be our friend, princess or no princess.'

Mistress Odette's face was pale, and she drummed her fingers on her desk in a worried manner. There was a big man standing behind her, dressed in the uniform of the Special Royal Guards. His pet tiger was so fierce-looking that even Mr Melchior was rather scared.

'I have arranged for you to be allowed a visit to see Princess Ursula this morning,' Mistress Odette said. 'I am sure it will help her to settle in.'

'Settle in?' Laura-Bella spoke up. 'But she's not going to stay there forever, is she?'

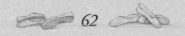

Mistress Odette said nothing. 'So, girls, you are to go to the King and Queen's private rooms at once,' she said. 'You will be given ten minutes to speak to Ursula.'

'*Ten measly minutes!*' exclaimed Val, as the Special Royal Guard and his tiger led them away. 'I shall have a thing or two to say to Ursula about that, let me tell you.'

But Valentina fell very silent as they were shown into the private part of the

Palace. They walked through long, endless corridor after long, endless corridor, each one even more beautifully decorated than the last. Every surface was made from solid gold, dotted with sparkling Frosting-Stones. Even the floors were made of gold. All around them, golden mirrors reflected their nervous faces.

'Stop!' said the Special Royal Guard so suddenly that they all bumped into each other. He knocked three times on a golden door, which opened.

'Send them in!' came Queen Mab's voice.

Trying hard to stop their knees knocking together, the girls and their pets all went through the door into a richly decorated bedroom. There were golden floors here too, and soft pink rugs, and a huge four-poster bed with pink and gold curtains.

Queen Mab was sitting on a very large chair by the window, and beside

her, on a smaller chair, were Ursula and Dorothea.

Ursula was wearing a long, pink gown. Her normally messy dark hair was curled in beautiful ringlets, topped off with a glittering Frosting-Stone tiara. Dorothea wore a small tiara too, and looked very uncomfortable in it.

'Ah, your friends, Princess Ursula. How nice,' said Queen Mab, looking as though she thought it was not nice in the slightest.

The girls all swept into their best curtseys and tried to grin at Ursula. But Ursula just looked away, out of the window.

'The Princess is about to start her embroidery lesson,' said the Queen, feeding her chubby eagle an Iced White Chocolate Drop from a large and expensive gold box, 'so you may not stay for long.'

'Oh, but Ursula . . . I mean, Princess

Ursula is already very good at sewing,' said
Jessica. 'She sews all her own ballet shoe
ribbons on and everything. We all do.'

Queen Mab stared at Jessica. 'That

may be, little Rock girl. But embroidery is a much finer skill. Besides, the Princess does not need to know how to sew ballet shoe ribbons on. She is not going to be a Ballerina.'

'But that's what she came to Ballet School for,' said Valentina.

'Ballet School is not at all suitable for a member of the Royal Family,' said the Queen, patting Ursula on the head. 'She will not be coming back next term.'

'But Ursula wants to be a Ballerina

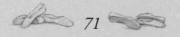

more than anything! Don't you, Ursula?' Jessica tried to talk to her friend, but Ursula still looked away, saying nothing.

'I think this visit has lasted long enough,' sighed the Queen. 'Guard, please take these girls away.'

'Great! Now we're *bound* to be executed,' wailed Sinbad, as they were all hustled from the chamber and back along the corridors. 'Or eaten alive,' he added, as the Special Royal Guard's tiger let out a growl.

'We won't be executed,' said Jessica, watching the golden doors slam shut behind them. 'But I don't think we're ever going to see Ursula and Dorothea again.'

CHAPTER FIVE
A Farewell to Ursula?

Later that day, Mistress Odette could not give the girls any good news.

'Queen Mab has made it clear that no more visits will be allowed,' she said, looking upset herself. 'There are even

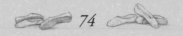

Special Royal Guards beneath Ursula's bedroom window.'

Sinbad began to wail loudly, as the others stared at the headmistress.

'But we'll never see her again . . .' began Crys.

'One day . . . perhaps . . . she'll be allowed to come out of the Palace,' said Mistress Odette, staring sadly across her desk at them. 'That is all I can promise you for now. The King and Queen lost their only daughter. They are going to be very careful not to lose their long-lost granddaughter, too.'

The girls and their pets shuffled out of the office, heads hanging low.

'This is a miserable little party, and no mistake!' said a voice nearby.

It was Master Silas, swishing along the corridor in his long, midnight blue cloak.

'We've just had terrible news about Ursula!' Sinbad burst out. 'She's got to be a hoity-toity princess up in the palace,

and we'll never ever see her or Dorothea again!'

'That is bad news,' said Master Silas softly. 'If Ursula was a friend of mine, I'm

not sure I'd put up with it.'

'But what can we do?' Laura-Bella asked. 'We're not allowed into the Palace to see her, and there are Special Royal Guards beneath her window, and –'

'Ah, yes, the guards,' said Master Silas. 'Very bad-tempered, those Special Royal Guards, I must say. I'm sure they'd be very annoyed if, shall we say, a very loud, rather naughty donkey shouted rude things at them. Why, they'd probably chase after him and leave the window unguarded for several minutes at least . . .'

Whistling to himself, he swished away down the corridor.

'Strange man,' said Valentina.

'Don't you see? He gave us an idea for how to speak to Ursula!' Jessica was already running off down the corridor. 'Come on!'

They crouched down in a thick patch of Daffodaisies in the gardens, from where they could see the two

Special Royal Guards outside Ursula's window.

'They're awfully big and cross-looking,' whispered Laura-Bella.

'And I don't much like the look of those tigers,' said Sinbad.

'Oh, they're big and grumpy all right,' said Mr Melchior. 'But they can't run as fast as a small tiger like me.'

Sinbad did not look comforted. 'But can they run as fast as a donkey?'

They quickly formed a plan.

Sinbad, with the loudest voice, would shout the rudest things he could possibly think of. Mr Melchior and Pollux, the swiftest runners, would appear from the bushes and make the guards and their tigers think it was they who had shouted rude things. While the guards chased them, Olympia the eagle would fly up to Ursula's window and get her attention so that the four girls could call up to her from below.

'Good luck, everyone,' said Jessica, squeezing her friends' hands.

Sinbad popped his head over the Daffodaisies and blew the loudest, rudest raspberry he could in the direction of the guards.

'Hey!' he yelled, as loudly as only a donkey could. 'You two porkers! You're so funny-looking, I bet you broke the bathroom mirror when you looked in it this morning!'

The guards' heads turned towards

the Daffodaisies.

Sinbad ducked down and shouted even louder. 'And you mangy old pair of tigers,' he brayed. 'When did you last wash behind your ears?'

Mr Melchior and Pollux bolted out of the shrubbery, waving their tails naughtily. Angrily, the guards and their tigers shot off after them.

'I hope they're all right,' Crys panted, as the four girls climbed out of the flower-patch.

'Don't worry,' said Laura-Bella. 'Mr Melchior can out-run anyone, and Pollux is wily enough to climb up trees if he has to.'

'Go on, Olympia,' said Valentina, letting her eagle go. 'Fly up to that window and get Ursula's –'

She stopped. All four of them were staring up at Ursula's bedroom window, which was already starting to open. A person was clambering out, clinging on to a thin rope, and making her way down

to the ground. It was Ursula.

'Ursula!' hissed Jessica. 'What are you doing?' Then, 'Be careful!' she added, with a shriek, as Ursula turned around to see who was there and almost let go of her rope in her astonishment.

'Hello!' Ursula waved at them all, her face breaking into a huge beam. 'I'm so glad to see you!'

They all ran forward, waiting to catch her if she fell, but just a couple of minutes later she was safely on the ground. She hugged them all so hard that her Frosting-Stones tiara fell off.

'I was watching those guards out of the window all day. I thought they'd never leave, but suddenly they did.' Ursula showed them her rope. 'I plaited together all my embroidery thread as soon as the Queen went off to lunch!'

'The guards have chased after Mr Melchior and Pollux. That was our plan. We just wanted to talk to you,' Jessica said, 'because we don't think we'll ever see you again now that you're a princess.'

'I'm not going to be a princess,' said Ursula. 'So that's that.'

Now it was their turn to be astonished. 'What do you mean?'

'Well, the King was terribly kind to me, and even the Queen meant to be nice, but I don't want to live with them in the Palace, away from my dad. And I don't want to learn how to be a proper princess – I want to learn how to be a

Ballerina, and stay at school with you.'
Ursula shook her ringlets so that they
were messy again. 'I've left the King and
Queen a note, telling them everything.
They're my grandparents, after all, so I
hope they'll understand. I just want to
live an ordinary life, at school and in
the Forest, with my dad and my
friends.'

'Your dad!' Crys remembered.
'Chancellor Goodfellow is holding him
prisoner!'

Ursula let out a giggle. 'You know, being a royal princess may not be all it's made out to be, but it comes in handy for this kind of thing. Chancellor Goodfellow has to obey every command I give him, so I'll just command him to let my dad go.'

'I want to be a princess,' said Sinbad, who had managed to put Ursula's tiara on his head. 'You get these really great hats and everyone has to do what you say.'

The girls hurried back into the school, where a very breathless Mr Melchior and Pollux were waiting for them in the Common Room. They had managed to lose the Special Royal Guards and their tigers somewhere in the Winter Garden. Then they all hurried straight to Mistress Odette's office. To their amazement, Chancellor Goodfellow was already there.

'Oh, girls!' Mistress Odette was looking dreadfully upset. 'I've tried to persuade the Chancellor to let Ursula's father go, but I'm afraid to say that I have failed.'

'But I'm sure I will succeed,' said

Ursula, in her quiet voice, stepping forward.

'Princess Ursula!' gasped Mistress Odette, sweeping a curtsey.

'Princess Ursula,' snapped the Chancellor, forcing himself to bow.

'Chancellor, I would like you to set my father free at once,' said Ursula.

'Command him to do something else, too,' whispered Sinbad. 'Make him recite his twelve times table, or do a polka, or stuff cream cakes in his ears, or something.'

'If he lets my dad go, that will be enough,' Ursula whispered back.

Chancellor Goodfellow squirmed and fidgeted, and looked as if he would like to imprison them all. 'As you wish, Princess Ursula.'

Off he stalked, angrily swinging a large bunch of keys. Only a few minutes later, a guard returned with Ursula's father.

He looked tired and rather grubby,

but he was so happy to see Ursula that he had tears in his eyes.

'I'm sorry that all this has happened,' he said, giving Ursula an enormous hug. 'And I'm sorry I never told you who your mother really was.'

'I don't mind about any of that, Daddy,' whispered Ursula, hugging him back. 'We're back together now, and that's all that matters. Anyway, now I understand lots of things, like why you never wanted to come to visit me at school.'

Her father smiled. 'I've wanted to come and see you dance ever since you started here. But it wasn't until I got that letter from those friends of yours that I knew I couldn't miss another chance. They were very firm on the matter!'

Ursula's friends all coughed, and shuffled their feet, and looked at the floor.

'I hoped no one would notice me,'

Ursula's father continued. 'But young Silas recognised me the minute he saw me.'

'Young Silas?' asked Ursula, surprised to hear stern Master Silas spoken of in this way.

'He was a young dancer at the Palace Theatre when I was in the orchestra,' her father explained. 'And he became a good friend. In fact, he used to carry notes between me and your mother. I should have known he would realise it was me, even after all these years. But I did hope that your grandparents would not be so quick!'

Suddenly, he stopped talking. The sound of the musical eagles was coming from out in the corridor.

'The King and Queen!' Mistress Odette whispered. 'Curtsey, girls!'

Jessica and the others exchanged nervous glances as the King and Queen swept into the room. Queen Mab was very pink in the face, and her Frosting-

Stone tiara was lopsided.

'Princess Ursula!' shrieked the Queen. 'How dare you run away like that, just when it was time for your History of Royalty lesson!'

'I was rather looking forward to showing you the family portraits, my dear,' added King Caspar, while his eagle flapped a friendly wing over at Dorothea. 'I thought it might be . . . er . . . good fun.'

Ursula took a deep breath. 'That

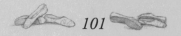

sounds as though it would be good fun, Grandfather,' she said. 'But could we do that another time? I've really missed my dad, you see. And my friends . . .'

Queen Mab let out a shriek so loud that everyone jumped. 'Ursula, you are a princess now! Princesses do not spend time with ordinary folk like this . . .'

'Hey!' Sinbad hissed in Jessica's ear. 'Who's she calling ordinary?'

'. . . and as for this Blue-Eyed Forest Dweller,' Queen Mab continued, staring

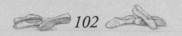

at Ursula's father as though he ought to be swept up with the rubbish, 'he may be your father, Ursula, but he has no idea how to bring up a princess . . .'

'But that's just it. I don't want to be a princess!' Ursula raised her voice.

The entire room fell silent.

'Grandfather, Grandmother, I know you only want me to be happy,' Ursula continued. 'And I'd love to come and stay with you at the Palace sometimes, and look at the family portraits, and even learn fine embroidery, if I must. But my home is back in the Forest, with Dad, and here at the Ballet School, with my friends. Can't I be Princess Ursula some of the time, and ordinary Ursula most of the time?'

Ursula's friends, her father and Mistress Odette all stared at her. They had never heard her say so much in one go before, let alone in front of the King and Queen.

As for the King and Queen, their mouths had fallen open.

'You mean you would rather stay at Ballet School than sit about and eat chocolates like a proper princess?' gasped Queen Mab.

'Yes,' said Ursula. 'Dancing means everything to me, Grandmother. Without ballet, I'm just not Ursula.'

'And you would rather live in a little tree-house in the Forest than live in splendour in our golden Palace?' King

Caspar asked.

'Yes,' said Ursula.

'Mad,' muttered Valentina and Sinbad, rolling their eyes.

Ursula walked over to the King, and put her hand through his. 'You should come and visit our tree-house, Grandfather. I think you'd like it.'

'Do you know, I . . . er . . . think I would!' said the King.

'Caspar!' shrieked the Queen. 'What are you saying?'

'Oh, you can come too, Grandmother,' said Ursula. 'Dorothea and Daddy and I will make it ever so comfortable for you. Won't we?'

Dorothea nodded, and Ursula's father could not help the smile on his face.

'Of course we will,' he said, bowing low to the Queen. 'It would be an honour.'

'Well!' said Queen Mab, straightening her tiara. 'Well!'

And she did not seem to know what else to say.

'We shall look forward to our visit!' said King Caspar, with a wide beam.

'Won't we, Mab, dear?'

'I suppose we shall,' murmured Queen Mab.

'Of course, we have some very important guests who must come to stay first,' said Ursula's father.

'Oh, yes!' said Ursula happily, turning to her friends in the corner. 'Will you all come for a holiday?'

'Try and stop us!' said Jessica.

And so, on the last day of term, Ursula, Jessica, Crys, Laura-Bella,

Valentina and all their pets packed their bags and set off for a week's holiday in the deep, dark, cool, green Forest. They swam in the stream and built tree-houses, and sat around the fire every night while Sinbad told them all long, spooky stories, filled to the brim with goblins and pirate ships.

'This has been the best week of my whole, entire life,' said Jessica, before they went to sleep in their tree-house on the last night of their holiday.

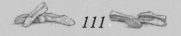

'And all the better,' said Ursula,
'when we know we'll be back at Ballet
School next year.'

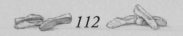

The End

Dorothea Sings Us The Royal Ballet School Song

From the Rocks we dancers come,

From the Rocks so high and steep.

Maybe with a donkey chum,

Maybe with a goat or sheep.

Though the journey takes a while,

Though the journey's tough and long,

On our way, we wear a smile,

On our way, we sing this song.

CHORUS

Ballerinas stick together
Fair or foul or any weather.
On this fact you may depend:
Here you'll always have a friend

From the Lake, we girls were chosen,
From the Lake, we make our way.
And, because our home is frozen,
Make the trip without delay.
On we stride, with bags and boxes,
Warmed by breaks for sardine stew,

Bringing with us Arctic foxes,
Baby seals and penguins, too.

CHORUS

In the Valley, you will find us
Basking in the hazy sun.
But we've left the warmth behind us,
Travelled north for dance and fun.
Leaving home, we're never tearful –
Monkeys join us on our way,
Tigers, too – but don't be fearful:
Tigers' friends are never prey.

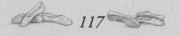

CHORUS

Forest Dwellers seldom chat,

Listening, we're more at ease.

Those who speak of this and that

Miss the music of the trees.

Leaving home is hard to do

But our Forest's always there.

And it's better two by two,

With a leopard or a bear.

CHORUS

In the City, traders hustle,

People run and people shout.

For this is the noise and bustle

Silverberg is all about.

But we've left behind those clatters,

Climbed this hill and reached this dome.

Ballet school is all that matters,

With our eagles, here we're home.

CHORUS

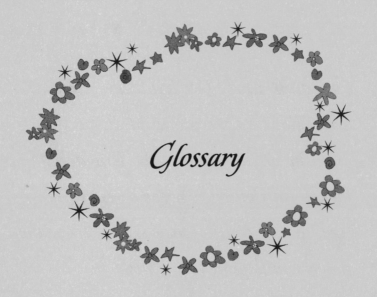

Glossary

Cinnamon Twists: Long, thin doughnuts that are twisted into a double knot before being freshly fried and then sprinkled with cinnamon sugar. A speciality of Silverberg. Donkeys love them.

Crocodils and Daffodaisies: Crocodils are yellow or purple wild flowers that grow in spring all over the Kingdom. In fact, wild flowers is a good description — like the crocodiles they sound like, the flowers will give you a little nip on the hand if you try to pick them before they are ready. Daffodaisies are less dangerous. They are tall white-and-yellow daisies the size of daffodils, and perfect for making into long Daffodaisy chains.

Frosting-Stones: Precious stones mined from the Frosty Mountains themselves. They come in several colours — red, green, blue and a deep amber — but the most prized of all are the colourless stones, more beautiful even than our own diamonds. The stones come out of the mountain just as they are, with no need for cutting or polishing. Finding a particularly large Frosting-Stone could make your fortune, but mining them is dangerous and difficult work.

Hot Buttered Flumpets: These are a little bit like the crumpets you eat for tea, but they taste softer and slightly sweeter, and they are shaped like fingers. They are always served piping hot, with melted butter oozing through the holes.

Ice Buns: Made for special occasions in the Lakes, these buns look plain on the outside but are filled with creamy pink-and-white ice cream on the inside. Be careful when you bite in!

Iced White Chocolate Drops: An expensive treat that only the very rich can afford. These chocolate drops are found by divers inside seashells at the very bottom of the northern Lake. They stay ice-cold right up until they are popped into your mouth, where they slowly melt.

Icicle Bicycles: Quite simply, bicycles carved from blocks of ice. They are the best way to travel from one side of the

frozen Lake to the other, as the icy wheels speed you across without any danger of skidding or slipping. But be warned, and pack a cushion – or the icy seat will leave your bottom extremely cold.

Lemon Fizzicles: Lemon-flavoured chewy sweets that fizz with tiny bubbles when you suck them.

Raspberry Flancakes: Flancakes are yeasty, flaky pancakes that rise up to five

or ten centimetres thick when you cook them in a special Flancake pan. Their outside is brown and rich with butter, their inside light and airy. Flancakes can be made in any flavour, but raspberry is the most popular. Donkeys love them, too.

Scoffins: Halfway between a scone and a muffin. They are best served fresh from the oven, split in two, and spread with Snowberry Jam.

Snowberries: Round, plump, juicy berries that grow in hedgerows all over the Kingdom throughout the winter. The snowberries from the south and the west are very dark pink, while the ones that grow in the east and the north are red in colour. Snowberries are always eaten cooked – in jams, Flancakes, waffles or muffins – where they taste sweet but tart at the same time. Don't make the mistake of eating one straight from the hedgerow, however tasty it looks. Uncooked

Snowberries are delicious, but they pop open in your mouth and fill it with a juice so sticky that your teeth are instantly glued together. This can take a whole morning to wear off.

Spring Sprung Day: The official first day of spring, and a big day for the inhabitants of the Kingdom after a long, cold winter. SpringSprung Day is marked with a big festival in Silverberg, but the Valley Dwellers throw parties in

their own homes for those who would rather not travel the long way to the City. For many, the highlight of the festivities is the SpringSprung Pudding (see below), though many delicious delicacies are served, including lemon-and-orangeade.

SpringSprung Pudding: A sponge pudding, filled with plump currants and chewy dried Snowberries, this is steamed in a huge pudding basin and served in thick slices, sprinkled with sugar, on

SpringSprung Day. One pudding will normally feed ten hungry people. Sinbad can eat a whole pudding all by himself, with room for afters.

Toffee Apple Torte: The speciality of the Grand Café and Tea-Rooms in Silverberg. This tart is made with delicate slices of the fruits that grow in the toffee-apple orchards in the deep south of the Valley, then served warm with toffee-butter sauce.

Who's Who in the Kingdom of the Frosty Mountains

The girls and their pets

Jessica Juniper – *Ballerina from the western Rocks*

Sinbad – *Jessica's pet donkey*

Crystal Coldwater –
*Ballerina from the northern
Lake*

Pollux – *Crystal's pet
white fox*

Laura-Bella Bergamotta –
*Ballerina from the
southern Valley*

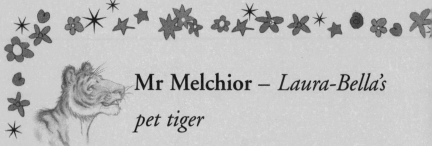

Mr Melchior – *Laura-Bella's pet tiger*

Ursula of the Boughs – *Ballerina from the eastern Forest*

Dorothea – *Ursula's pet bear*

Valentina de la Frou – *Ballerina from the City*

 Olympia – *Valentina's pet eagle*

Some other Ballerinas

Rubellina Goodfellow – *Ballerina from the City, and the Chancellor's daughter*

Jo-Jo Marshall – *Another Ballerina from the City, and Rubellina's best friend*

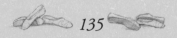

The Teachers

Mistress Odette – *the Headmistress*

Mistress Camomile – *a Ballet teacher*

Master Lysander – *another Ballet teacher, also known as Mustard Stockings*

Master Silas – *the History of Ballet teacher*

Mistress Hawthorne – *the Gym teacher*

Mistress Babette – *the Costume, Hair and Make-up teacher*

Master Jacques – *the Mime teacher*

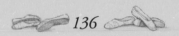

The Royal Party

King Caspar – *the King*

Queen Mab – *the Queen*

Chancellor Godwin Goodfellow – *the Kingdom's Chancellor*

Don't miss the first book in the series

It's Jessica's first day at Ballet School
and she wants to make a good
impression. So when the teachers think
she has played a practical joke on the
High Minister's daughter, Jessica and
Sinbad the donkey have to try extra hard.
But things keep going wrong.
Can Jessica prove her innocence?

**Twinkle your toes with the Ballerinas
and their talking pets!**

KINGDOM OF THE FROSTY MOUNTAINS

Jessica Juniper

by
Emerald Everhart

Inside the perfume bottle
a magical kingdom is waiting for you ...

Don't miss the second book in the series

The Ballerinas-in-Training are excited –
they have to write about their favourite
ballerina, Eva Snowdrop. So why is Crys
so upset? Even her fox, Pollux, can't
soothe her. Can the girls find out? And
how will Icicle Bicycles help?

**Twinkle your toes with the Ballerinas
and their talking pets!**

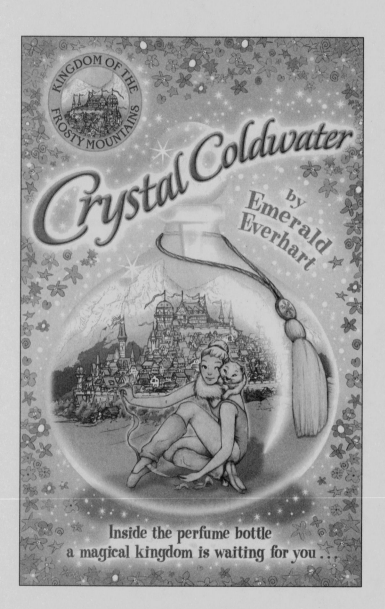

KINGDOM OF THE FROSTY MOUNTAINS

Crystal Coldwater

by
Emerald
Everhart

Inside the perfume bottle
a magical kingdom is waiting for you . . .

Don't miss the third book in the series

It's SpringSprung time and everyone in
Silverberg is preparing for the Festival.
But Laura-Bella and Mr Melchior the
tiger aren't in the mood to celebrate.
They need to save their family farm.
Their friends want to help, but it means
disobeying the Ballet School rules . . .

**Twinkle your toes with the Ballerinas
and their talking pets!**

KINGDOM OF THE
FROSTY MOUNTAINS

Laura-Bella

by
Emerald
Everhart

Inside the perfume bottle
a magical kingdom is waiting for you ...

Don't miss the fourth book in the series

Valentina's mother has decided to
send Valentina to another school.
But Val and Olympia the eagle don't
want to leave their friends. Olympia
would miss her hero, Sinbad the donkey,
desperately. Besides, they love ballet!
Can the girls help Val
prove she deserves to stay?

**Twinkle your toes with the Ballerinas
and their talking pets!**

KINGDOM OF THE FROSTY MOUNTAINS

Valentina de la Frou

by
Emerald
Everhart

Inside the perfume bottle
a magical kingdom is waiting for you . . .

EGMONT PRESS: ETHICAL PUBLISHING

Egmont Press is about turning writers into successful authors and children into passionate readers – producing books that enrich and entertain. As a responsible children's publisher, we go even further, considering the world in which our consumers are growing up.

Safety First
Naturally, all of our books meet legal safety requirements. But we go further than this; every book with play value is tested to the highest standards – if it fails, it's back to the drawing-board.

Made Fairly
We are working to ensure that the workers involved in our supply chain – the people that make our books – are treated with fairness and respect.

Responsible Forestry
We are committed to ensuring all our papers come from environmentally and socially responsible forest sources.

For more information, please visit our website at
www.egmont.co.uk/ethicalpublishing